STAR WARS
GALAXY OF CREATURES

DISCARDED

Written by Kristin Baver

DISNEY
LUCASFILM
P R E S S

LOS ANGELES · NEW YORK

This is SF-R3, but you can call
him Aree.

Aree is a member of the Galactic Society of Creature Enthusiasts.

Aree travels the galaxy on his ship with his friend, Cam.
Aree must be brave to learn all about wildlife, creatures both big and small.

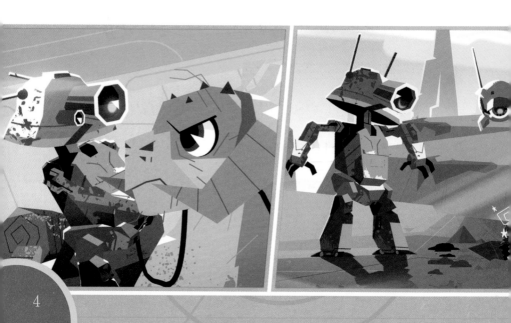

Aree must be smart to befriend
the beasts he meets.
And sometimes Aree must be fast
to outrun danger.
Good thing he was built to
explore!

On the planet Hoth, Aree found a tauntaun.

Aree's mission was to tame and control the beast.

Learning to ride the creature was
harder than Aree expected.
But it was nothing to lose his
head over.
And Aree soon learned that
tauntauns love jogan fruit pie.

Wampas are white as snow.
On Hoth, they are the tauntaun's
natural enemy.

But the wampa Aree discovered
was sick with a cold!
He had a sneeze that could cause
an avalanche.

Aree tried giving the creature a hot bath.

He made the wampa rootleaf stew.

He started a campfire to warm the creature's chilly cave.

But the cure was to cool down the wampa's fever with snow.
A cold wampa is a happy wampa!
And a hungry wampa.
Good thing wampas don't eat droids.

On Dathomir, Aree met a rancor.
Like wampas, rancors are fierce
meat eaters.
But this one needed help.
Building up his courage, Aree
took a look inside the rancor's
stinky mouth.

Aree began cleaning the
creature's sharp teeth.
It was hard, smelly work.
With help from a flock of birds,
soon the rancor's teeth were
gleaming.

On Tatooine, Aree met a herd of banthas.
The furry creatures were in need of a bath.
Some Tusken Raiders showed Aree how to help clean the beasts.

Aree combed the beast's fur.
He gave his bantha a special style.
Aree discovered that with some
elbow grease and ribbons,
a bantha could be beautiful.

On Endor, Aree met a pen full of blurrgs!

The tough-skinned creatures eat grass, weeds, and sometimes each other.

Aree crashed into the fence and accidentally set the blurrgs free.

He tried to keep the herd
together by flying circles around
them. It didn't work.
Then he whistled a tune, and the
blurrgs followed his song.

In the deadly jungle of Cholganna, Aree met a nexu perched on a nest made of bones.
With four eyes and sharp teeth, quills, and claws, the creature was very scary at first.

But Aree discovered the nexu was just protecting her babies. When he saw poachers try to trap her, Aree rushed to help and made a new friend along the way.

On Naboo, Aree met a voorpak.
The furry creatures with six long,
thin legs are popular pets.
Aree wondered if they could also
be trained to protect.

The animal was more interested in chasing insects and playing with Cam.

You can't always change a creature's nature.

The voorpak is nice to cuddle but doesn't make a good guard.

On the grassy world of Lothal,
Aree found an orphaned Loth-cat.
The pointy-eared creatures hunt
for Loth-rats in the wild.
But Loth-cats can also be very
picky eaters.
Very picky.

This Loth-cat only ate what he wanted to eat.

He only played when he wanted to play.

He only slept where he wanted to sleep. What a picky kitty!

On the rocky world of Elphrona,
Aree met a friendly charhound.
These doglike creatures have
fiery breath.

Aree wondered: Do charhounds
like to play fetch?

Aree tried throwing the charhound pieces from his ship, but they all went up in smoke! Only fireproof crystals from Elphrona were safe enough for play.

The charhound wasn't the only creature that was tough on Aree's ship.
After landing on an asteroid, Aree and Cam found a group of mynocks.

The winged creatures feed on
energy.
They feasted on the ship's power
lines.
Aree was next on the menu!
Luckily, Aree and Cam escaped
before it was lights-out!

On Kowak, Aree and Cam hoped
to find Kowakian monkey-lizards,
who love to laugh.
As soon as their ship landed,
monkey-lizards began tearing the
craft apart!

It turns out monkey-lizards love to pick apart machines.
Luckily, their attention soon went back to laughing instead.
After that, they agreed to help fix Aree's ship.

On Batuu, Aree met some curious porgs.

The wide-eyed birds watched Aree as he tried to train them with a clicker.

The flock of porgs were not interested in learning tricks. But they did teach Aree how to survive a braga bear attack!

In a galaxy of creatures, Aree
learned that all critters have a
purpose.
And whether big or small,
they should all be treated with
caution and care.